Disney · PIXAR

THE INCREDIBLES

Adapted by John Sazaklis
Illustrated by Don Clark

A GOLDEN BOOK • NEW YORK

 Published in the United States by Golden Books, an imprint of Random House Children's Books, a division of Penguin Random House LLC, 1745 Broadway, New York, NY 10019, and in Canada by Penguin Random House Canada Limited, Toronto, in conjunction with Disney Enterprises, Inc. Golden Books, A Golden Book, A Little Golden Book, the G colophon, and the distinctive gold spine are registered trademarks of Penguin Random House LLC.

rhcbooks.com

ISBN 978-0-7364-3863-6 (trade) — ISBN 978-0-7364-3864-3 (ebook)

Printed in the United States of America

10 9 8 7 6 5 4 3 2

It was the **GOLDEN AGE OF SUPERS**!

It was a time when heroes like **Mr. Incredible**, **Elastigirl**, and **Frozone** kept the world safe from all kinds of danger.

It was an exciting time!

Built like a tank and ten times as tough, Mr. Incredible was known for his **super strength**.

Elastigirl's **stretching abilities** made her as flexible as she was fierce.

They made a **POWERFUL** pair!

Then times changed. People complained that the Supers were making a mess of things. The government forced them into hiding.

Mr. Incredible and Elastigirl fell in love and got married. They tried to live normal lives. They became **Bob** and **Helen Parr**.

The Parrs moved to a house in the suburbs and raised a family. They had a daughter named **Violet**, a son named **Dash**, and a baby boy named **Jack-Jack**.

Like their parents, the kids were **Supers**!

Violet could **turn invisible** and **create force fields** . . .

. . . while Dash, true to his name, could **run really fast**! ***ZOOM!***

Jack-Jack's powers were still unknown. He wasn't even potty-trained!

Banned from showing their powers in public, Bob and Helen used them around the house instead.

But Bob was bored with being normal. He passed the time at his new job wishing he were still doing his old job—being a Super!

One day, his wish came true.

A mysterious woman named **Mirage** gave Bob a top-secret mission.

This was a job for Mr. Incredible!

Bob's supersuit had been damaged in battle. He visited fashion designer **Edna Mode** and asked her to make him a new one.

With his new supersuit, Mr. Incredible was back in business.

Mirage led him to a private island—and into a trap! Mr. Incredible was caught in the clutches of a robot known as the **Omnidroid**.

The trap had been set by an evil genius named **SYNDROME**.

As a boy, Syndrome wanted to be Mr. Incredible's sidekick. When that didn't happen, Syndrome became *very* angry.

Syndrome wanted revenge. He created high-tech gadgets to destroy Mr. Incredible with one day.

And that day was today!

When her husband didn't return home, a worried Helen visited Edna. Helen was shocked to learn that Bob was Mr. Incredible again—*and* that he was in terrible danger!

Luckily, Edna had made new supersuits for the entire Parr family. They were about to go on a rescue mission!

After leaving Jack-Jack with a sitter, Elastigirl set out to save Mr. Incredible. Violet and Dash secretly followed. They wanted to help, too!

Bob was happy to be reunited with his fantastic family. At that moment, they were no longer the Parrs. They were . . .

. . . THE INCREDIBLES!

Suddenly, the Incredibles were surrounded by Syndrome's soldiers.

Mr. Incredible **heaved** their hovercrafts high overhead.

Elastigirl **stretched** out to make several long-distance strikes.

Dash **ran** circles around the guards, and Violet trapped them in an unbreakable **force field**.

The Incredibles realized the best Super power of all was **teamwork**!

When the fight was over, the Incredibles raced to capture Syndrome. The villain was in a rocket headed toward the mainland. He was going to unleash the Omnidroid on the city.

The Incredibles would never make it there in time!

Fortunately, Mirage had a change of heart. She felt sorry for her part in Syndrome's plot and led the Supers to one of his spare rockets.

The Incredibles thanked her and were soon blasting off to their next battle.

When the Supers arrived, the Omnidroid was tearing up the town. Syndrome watched, cackling with glee.

The Incredibles tried everything to defeat the giant robot. Even with icy help from **Frozone**, the Omnidroid seemed unstoppable.

Then Violet saw that Syndrome was using a remote control to make the Omnidroid move.

The Supers stopped fighting the robot and went after Syndrome. They snatched the remote control and turned the Omnidroid against him. An energy beam blasted Syndrome out of the sky!

With Syndrome defeated, the heroes tricked the Omnidroid into destroying itself. The city was saved!

Citizens gathered to celebrate the return of the Supers.

The Supers felt good to be back.

They felt **INCREDIBLE**!